To my children, Ella and Iddo

Dear parents and readers,

One, Two, Family is a children's book also suitable for toddlers. It tells the story of one family comprising of a mother, a girl and a boy. This particular family is very much like most, in which more often than not there are two parents and one or more children, but it differs from most in that this is a single parent family.

The story told in this book is the story of many single parent families. It tries to answer questions that many children, and especially children of single parents, grapple with. Questions such as: "where did I come from?" or "Who brought me into this world?" and in particular "Why don't I have a Daddy?"

The issue of "have" and "have not" is one of the most central and complex issues faced by all families, and all the more so by single parent families. Children see the world through their parents' eyes, and when parents have a secure and positive attitude regarding their "haves" and "have nots", their children feel it and the world is then perceived by them as secure and positive both in areas that are full and in those areas that are lacking.

It is for this reason that dealing with this issue is so important. It facilitates a discussion between children and parents about those things with which we are blessed and those that we lack, about what we can or cannot achieve, while at the same time making it possible to express the entire gamut of emotions that may arise from such a discussion.

The story progresses along three levels. One may read the story in one sitting, from beginning to end, or one may read only specific chapters, appropriate to the child's age, level of understanding and patience, gradually adding the different sections so as to form a complete story.

In the first chapter we meet the family: Mother, Ella and Iddo. The issues dealt with in this chapter are: Introducing the members of the family, the activities they share, and how they may be and act together or separately. You can also engage the child in a discussion, asking questions such as, "what do I like to do with Mom or with Dad?", "What do I like to do by myself?", and "What do I like to do with others?"

The second chapter deals with bringing children into the world. It describes how Ella and Iddo came into the world without their mother having a partner. This chapter tries to answer the questions mentioned previously: "where did I come from?", "Who brought me into this world?" and in particular, "Why don't I have a Daddy?" In families with only one child, reading the part about bringing the child into the world once will suffice. If there is more than one child, it is recommended that each child be given their own story. This chapter also allows us to talk about what we can do, as children and as adults, to make positive changes in our lives.

The third and final chapter brings together the previous chapters and deals with the issues of "have" and "have not", the similar and the diverse, and the kinds of feelings that arise from them: "How my family is like or unlike other families?" This chapter offers further possibilities to talk about other things that "I have" or "I don't have", things I can achieve and what I lack and couldn't achieve, and also issues such as "how do I resemble my Mom or Dad and how am I different?" and "how am I like others and how am I different?"

I'd like to thank Nurit Yuval, the Illustrator and literary editor of my book, who unfailingly helped me complete all that was missing in the book. Rafi Moses, my copy editor, who so succinctly structured the book's musical tone. Orly Mazor-Yuval, my translator, who made it possible for the book to soar beyond the limits of my mother tongue, Hebrew. Sigalit Eshet, my graphic designer, who turned words and illustrations into a book. And my dear parents and children, without whom this book would not have been written.

In his book for educators, "How to Love a Child", Janusz Korczak writes: "The child has every right to demand respect for his grief, though it be but for the loss of a pebble, for his wish, though it be but a fancy to go for a walk without an overcoat in cold weather, for an apparently senseless question… God, what will you do to protect this sensitive soul so that life may not drag it in the mud?"

Yours

Michal Keidar, clinical social worker and psychotherapist

michala.keidar@gmail.com

Tel Aviv, Israel

One, Two, Family

By: Michal Keidar

Illustrations: Nurit Yuval

Hello,
I'm Ella and Iddo's mother
and I'd like to tell you
about Ella, Iddo
and our family.

When you come to our house,
you will see on our front door a sign
with a drawing of a house and three bears:
a big mamma bear,
a small girl-bear
and a little baby boy-bear.

So when you come to our house
you can tell that here live:
Mother: big,
Ella, the girl: small
and Iddo, the boy: little.

Iddo, Ella and mother's home

When you come into our house
you will also see we have
one room with a big bed:
Mother's room,
and a second room with two small beds:
Ella and Iddo's room.

Ella, Iddo and Mother
love to do all kinds of things together:
to read stories, to sing songs,
to play games, to tickle-tickle,
to swing on the swings, to slide down the slides,
to hug-hug, to kiss-kiss,
to get mad, to yell, to cry, to laugh,
to fight now and again
and then to make up.

Sometimes, Mother does things
only with Ella. For example:
Ella picks out a book, or two, or three,
and Mother will read them to her as bed time stories.

Sometimes, mother does things
only with Iddo. For example:
Mother lifts Iddo way up,
almost to the ceiling,
and tells him: "You're Superman",
and he laughs and laughs.

And sometimes,
Ella and Iddo do things together,
just the two of them, without Mother.
For example:
Ella cooks a tasty meal in the little play kitchen,
gives Iddo his food,
but he mainly just sucks on the spoon.

Sometimes, Mother does things all on her own,
for example:
She sits at the computer with a cup of coffee.

Sometimes, Ella does things all on her own,
for example:
She takes all the crayons out of their box
and draws a picture.

And sometimes,
Iddo does things all on his own,
for example:
He tries to get to one of the toys on the carpet
and put it in his mouth.

Ella and Iddo have a grandpa and a grandma,
who are Mother's parents.
Ella and Iddo also have uncles,
who are Mother's brothers.
Ella and Iddo also have cousins,
who are Mother's nephews.

And Ella and Iddo have a mother.
Ella has a brother: Iddo,
Iddo has a sister: Ella.
And this is our family:

Mother, Ella and Iddo.

Before Ella and Iddo were born,
I, Ella and Iddo's Mother,
was not Ella and Iddo's Mother.
I was a woman who had
a green car and a big bed
and a computer and lots and lots of books.
But I didn't have children.
And I really wanted children.
I really wanted Ella and Iddo.
I really wanted to be Ella and Iddo's Mother.

In order to have children you need eggs and sperm.
Women have eggs, and men have sperm.
I am a woman. I have eggs, but I don't have sperm.
In many families a woman and a man meet,
get to know each other and become friends.
They share the eggs and the sperm,
like good friends do.
I didn't have a boyfriend,
and I didn't have anyone to share my eggs with.

But I really wanted children.
I really wanted Ella and Iddo.
I really wanted to be Ella and Iddo's Mother.

So I went to the doctor and told him:
"Doctor, doctor, I really want children.
I really want to be Ella's Mother,
but I don't have any sperm.
Can you help me find some sperm?"
And the good doctor said:
"Certainly! Of course I can. I'd be glad to.
I have some wonderful sperm for you."
And I was very glad and said to him:
"Thank you so much, good doctor."

The good doctor
placed the wonderful sperm in my womb.
And my eggs
were very glad to meet the wonderful sperm.
They hugged one another really tight
until they became one cell, which became two,
and gradually
a whole bunch of cells grew in my womb,
and became an amazing baby-girl,
Ella.

Little Ella grew and grew in my womb,
And when she was good and ready, she was born.
And I was happy.

I had an amazing
baby-girl. Ella.
And I became a mother.
Ella's mother.

After I became Ella's mother,
I also wanted to be Iddo's mother.
I wanted Ella to have a brother,
and I wanted Iddo to have a sister.

So once again I went to the good doctor.
And once again I said to him:
"Good doctor, I really also want to be Iddo's mother.
I really want to be Ella and Iddo's mother.
Can you help me find
some more of that wonderful sperm?"
And the good doctor said:
"Certainly! Of course I can. I'd be glad to."
And I was very glad and said to him:
"Thank you so much, good doctor."

The good doctor
placed the wonderful sperm in my womb.
And my eggs
were very glad to meet the wonderful sperm.
They hugged one another really tight
until they became one cell, which became two,
and gradually
a whole bunch of cells again grew in my womb,
and became an amazing baby-boy,
Iddo.

Little Iddo grew and grew in my womb,
and when he was good and ready, he was born.
And I was happy. Again.
I already had an amazing baby-girl, Ella.
And now I had an amazing baby-boy, Iddo.

And I became
Ella and Iddo's mother.

There are families that have a father and a mother,
just as I, Ella and Iddo's mother,
have a father and a mother,
and they are Ella and Iddo's grandpa and grandma.
And sometimes we – Mother, Ella and Iddo –
are sad that there is no father in our family.
And that's OK.
It's alright to be sad
when you feel that something is missing.

But,
we have a family of our own:
Mother, Ella and Iddo.
And Grandpa and Grandma.
And uncles and aunties.
And cousins.
And we've also got lots of friends.

And we – Ella, Iddo and Mother–
love to do all kinds of things together:
to read stories, to sing songs,
to play games, to tickle-tickle,
to swing on the swings, to slide down the slides,
to hug-hug, to kiss-kiss,
to get mad, to yell, to cry, to laugh,
to fight now and again
and then to make up.

And we know that there are other families
with only a father or only a mother.
And any way,
There are all kinds of families.

39483634R00022

Made in the USA
San Bernardino, CA
27 September 2016